spot

MIGHTY MACHINES

FIRE TRUCKS

by Wendy Strobel Dieker

AMICUS | AMICUS INK

lights

locker

Look for these words and pictures as you read.

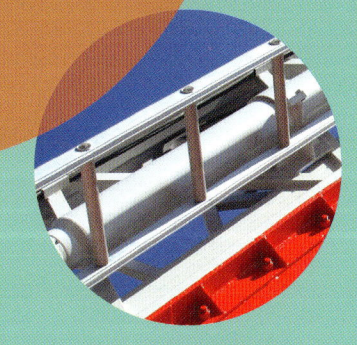

hose

ladder

A fire truck races by. What can it do?

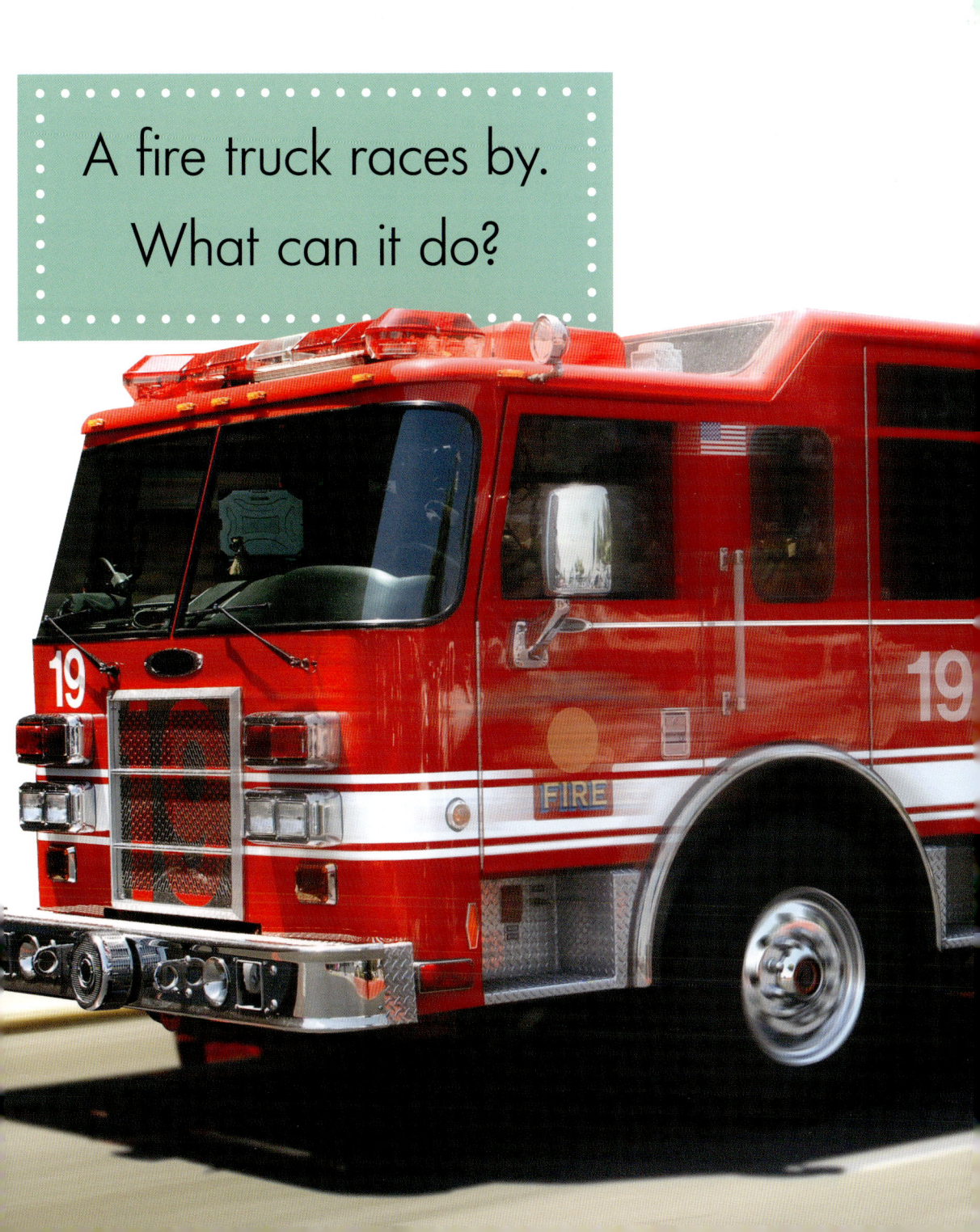

A fire truck takes fire fighters to a fire. It holds all their gear.

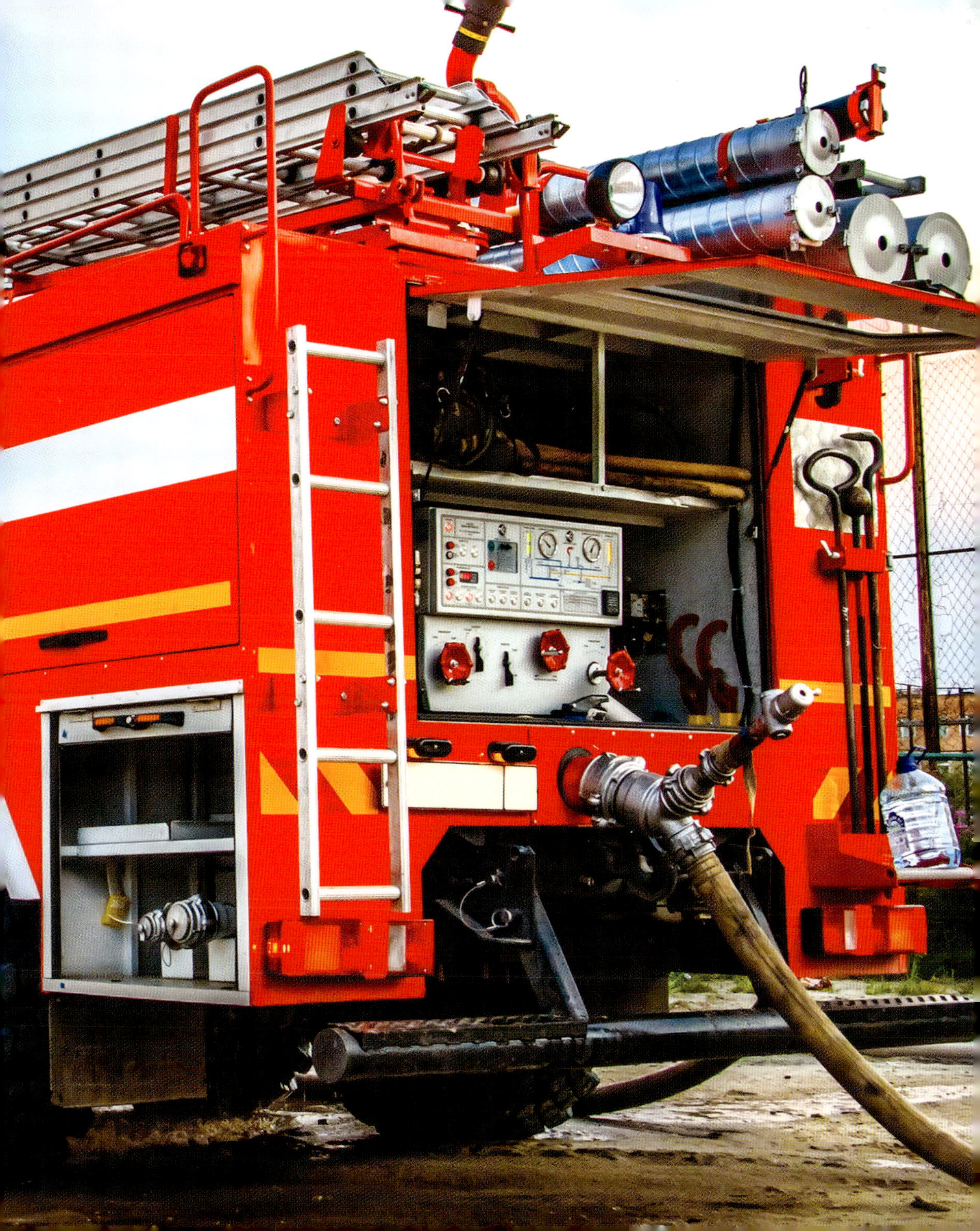

See the lights?
They warn cars to move.
The fire truck is in a hurry.

lights

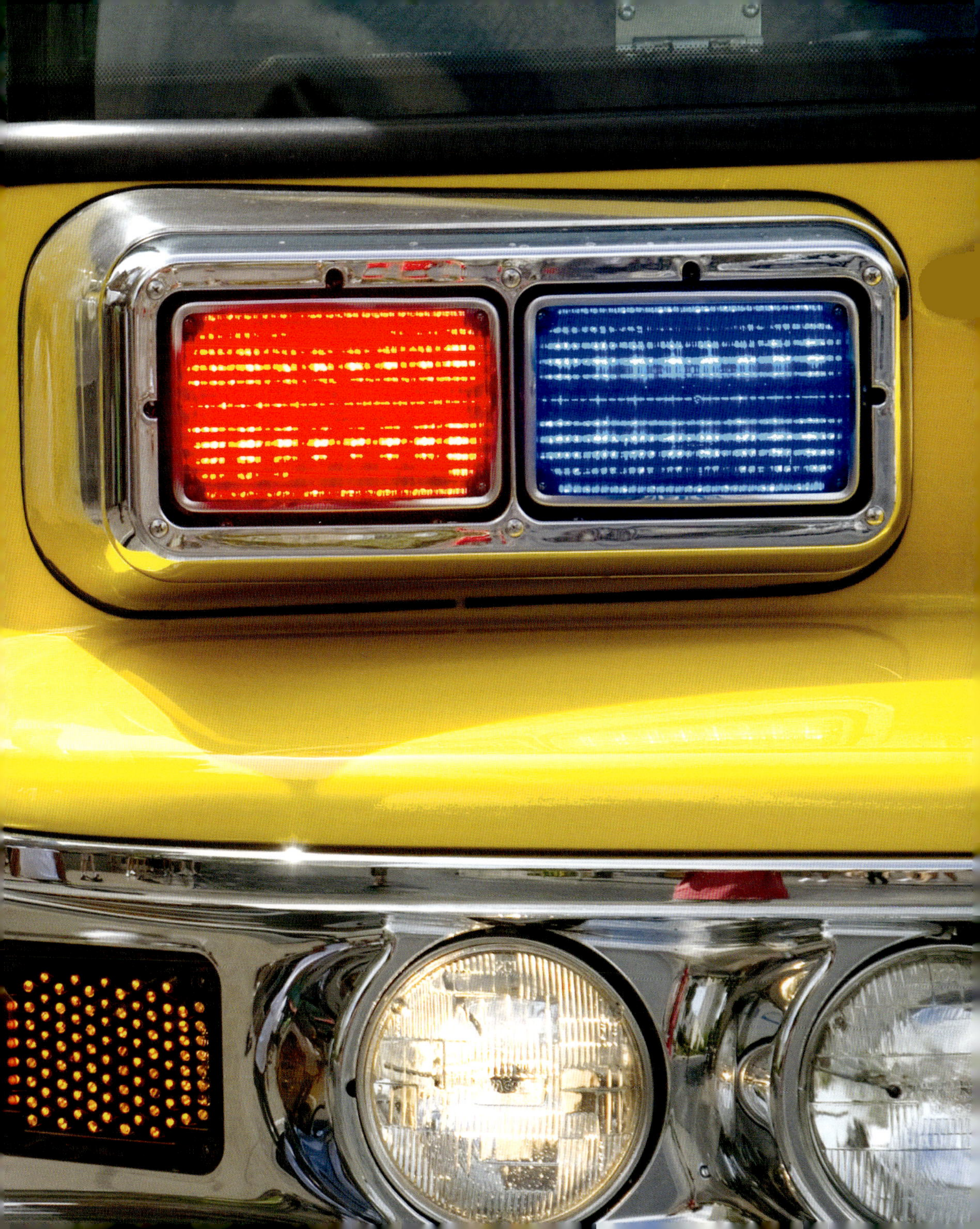

See the locker?
Tools are inside.
Each tool has a
special place.

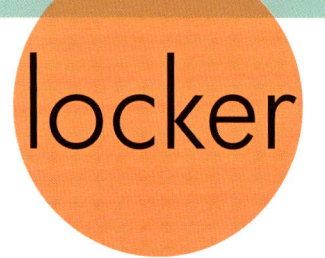

locker

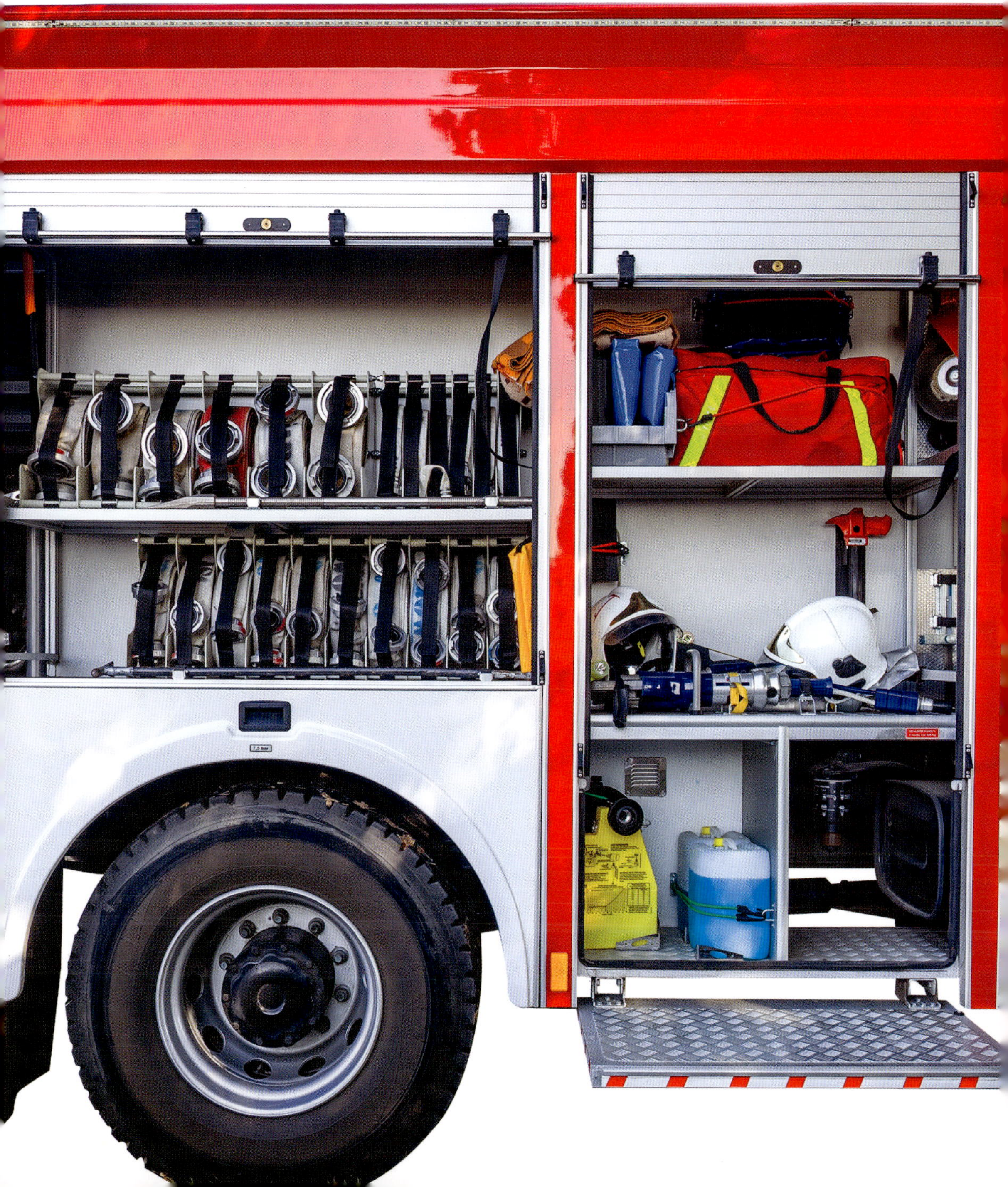

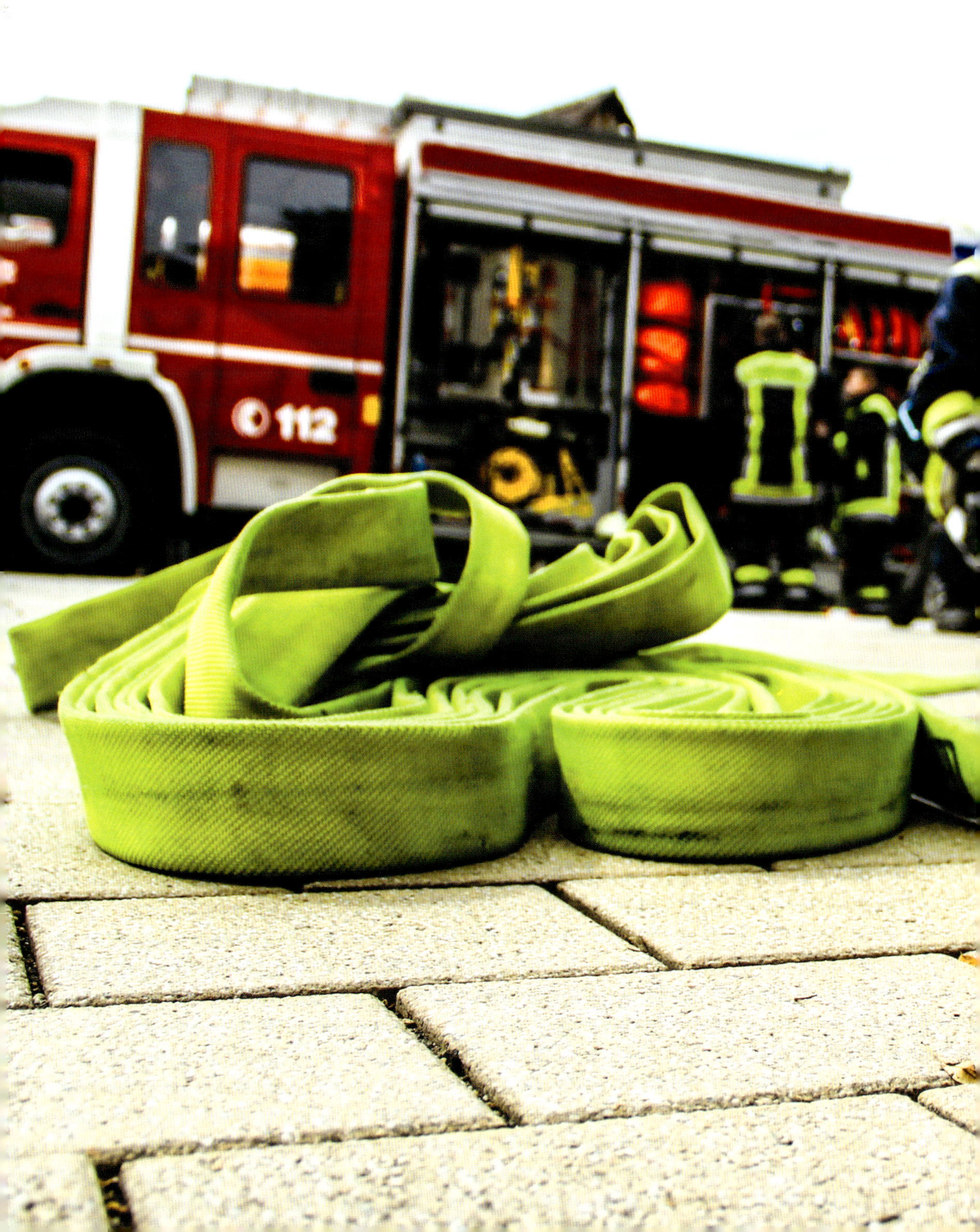
112

See the hose?
It hooks up to the fire hydrant.
It sprays water on the fire.

hose

See the ladder?
It goes up.
It spins around.

ladder

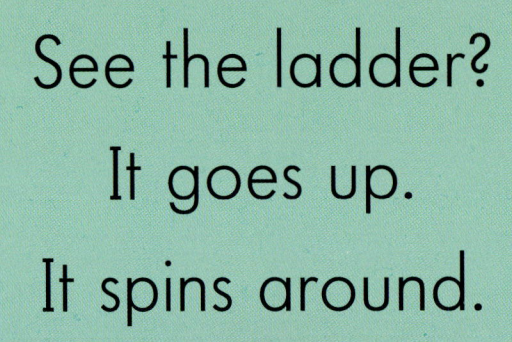

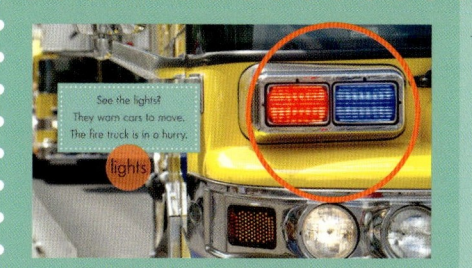

lights

locker

Did you find?

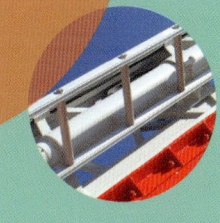

hose

ladder

Spot is published by Amicus and Amicus Ink
P.O. Box 1329, Mankato, MN 56002
www.amicuspublishing.us

Copyright © 2019 Amicus.
International copyright reserved in all countries.
No part of this book may be reproduced in any form
without written permission from the publisher.

Library of Congress Cataloging-in-Publication Data
Names: Dieker, Wendy Strobel, author.
Title: Fire trucks / by Wendy Strobel Dieker.
Description: Mankato, Minnesota : Amicus, [2019] |
Series: Spot. Mighty machines | Audience: K to Grade 3.
Identifiers: LCCN 2017033358 (print) | LCCN 2017054812
 (ebook) | ISBN 9781681514550 (pdf) | ISBN 9781681513737
 (library binding) | ISBN 9781681522937 (pbk.)
Subjects: LCSH: Fire engines--Juvenile literature. | Fire
 extinction--Equipment and supplies--Juvenile literature. | CYAC:
 Fire engines. | Fire extinction.
Classification: LCC TH9372 (ebook) | LCC TH9372 .D54 2019
 (print) | DDC 628.9/259--dc23
LC record available at https://lccn.loc.gov/2017033358

Printed in China

HC 10 9 8 7 6 5 4 3 2 1
PB 10 9 8 7 6 5 4 3 2 1

To my favorite mighty machine
drivers, Big Jerr and Smoke 'em
Joe —WSD

Rebecca Glaser, editor
Deb Miner, series designer
Aubrey Harper, book designer
Holly Young, photo researcher

Photos by Alamy Stock Photo/
Kumar Sriskandan, 2, 6-7, 15;
iStock/ryasick, 1, jgroup, 3,
DarthArt, 4-5, ewg3D, 2, 8-9,
15; klein_design_photography,
2, 10-11, 15, FrankvandenBergh,
14; Shutterstock/David Touchtone,
cover, 16, sspopov, 2, 12-13, 15

The fire truck is back at the station.
It is ready for the next fire.